Zista

Stories From India

Series II

Ukiyoto Publishing

All global publishing rights are held by
Ukiyoto Publishing

Published in 2024

Content Copyright © **Ukiyoto**

ISBN 9789364944830

All rights reserved.
No part of this publication may be reproduced, transmitted, or stored in a retrieval system, in any form by any means, electronic, mechanical, photocopying, recording or otherwise, without the prior permission of the publisher.

The moral right of the author has been asserted.

This is a work of fiction. Names, characters, businesses, places, events, locales, and incidents are either the products of the author's imagination or used in a fictitious manner. Any resemblance to actual persons, living or dead, or actual events is purely coincidental.

This book is sold subject to the condition that it shall not by way of trade or otherwise, be lent, resold, hired out or otherwise circulated, without the publisher's prior consent, in any form of binding or cover other than that in which it is published.

Zista represents Culture, the hub of which lies in India

This title holds in its pages the very essence of India, its people and its culture, conveyed through a selection of short stories by few of the best authors of India.

CONTENTS

The Eye   1
By Proma Nautiyal

Those Rusted Lines   11
By Pratyay Ganguly

The Walls Have Ears   36
By Manali Desai

About the Authors   *45*

The Eye

by Proma Nautiyal

Ranju, **beta** what's the time right now?

"*Maa*! Not again." Ranju said in his mind.

Looking at objects and ascertaining their positions around him had become a cumbersome task for Ranju, let alone spot the tiny two hands in the clock.

You see, the 8-year old was having some strange issues with his eyesight. It had been seven months since his vision started blurring. He had absolutely no idea as to why it was happening.

Ranju was scared to tell his mother about it.

"Staring at the sunlight all the time, eh Ranju? Now I will have to take you to an eye doctor. Do you even know how expensive the doctor's fee is? And then the medicines and treatment…how will I manage all this with this limited income? If only you would spare me all this trouble and not stare at the sun all the time. It's no friend of yours, Ranju! Why don't you just go and make some real friends?"

Ranju had been through this routine reprimand session multiple times already, and had no interest in going through it, again. Neither did he want a doctor poking and prodding at his eyeballs with some strange apparatus.

Between his limited idea about how treatments work and increasing issues of eyesight, Ranju decided the latter was better and would certainly heal on its own.

His habit of staring at the sun was not newfound. He had been doing this for years now. When he was three, Ranju's mother Sona introduced him to the giant ball of fire in the sky called 'the sun'. She explained to him the important role the sun played in nourishing all life on earth.

Ever since, he became mesmerized with the ball of fire. He would find the sun especially appealing when it would start looking like a *motichoor laddoo** just before it was about to set in the evening. You never know what a kid takes fancy to. It could be a stick, the neighbor's dog, grandma's glasses, and in Ranju's case, it was the sun.

The otherwise friendless Ranju found a friend, and a powerful one. One that did not fight with him, or make fun of his short and thin stature, or that his father had left the mother-son duo to chase an insane dream of becoming an actor in Bollywood. Manoranjan Kumar, as he was named at birth, did not really have any memories of his father. He was only two when their world of three turned into a world of two. The only gift he had received from his father was his name, Manoranjan, which means entertainment in Hindi. Why his father would name him 'Manoranjan' was pretty self explanatory given his love for the entertainment industry.

But for the little boy, life was far from entertaining. At eight, Ranju seemed to be trapped in the body of a five-year old. His mother felt utterly guilty about the fact that she wasn't able to provide enough food or nourishment to the apple of her eye. Sona worked as a handloom weaver in the village they lived in.

Olasingh was a tiny little village, about fifty kilometres away from the city, Bhubaneshwar, in Orissa. The net population of the village would be less than a hundred. As such, practically everyone knew everyone. This fact was both helpful and painful at the same time. However, people coexisted happily in the village sharing gossips and delicious *pakhala bhata* which is typically fermented rice and a true delicacy.

Sona was not originally from *Olasingh*. She came to the village as a young bride, with just a bag full of clothes and some light gold ornaments which were wedding gifts from her family. She did not have any education and had little skill when it came to the loom. There was no other way, she could have possibly sustained herself and her child in a village known for its textile outputs.

At twenty, Sona tucked her toddler in a makeshift baby carrier and headed for the looms. She learned fast. Soon, she was creating beautiful sarees, full six yards of it in just three to four days. She was now confident that she could at least feed her child rice, twice a day, and also manage to send him to school when he was of the right age. She wanted Ranju to study and become a white-collar job holder, even if it took her a million sarees to make that happen.

Initially, she had been putting every penny together to create a school and college fund for Ranju. But ever since Ranju started having issues with his eyesight, she started saving fastidiously, a penny at a time, to fund a visit to the eye doctor in the nearby town.

Ranju loved his mother as any child does. But even more so because she was the only family he had got. He was not your regular eight-year old. He didn't care about marbles and toy cars. He just had two peculiar habits: staring at the sun and sitting with his eyes closed. Nobody really understood Ranju or his bizarre habits and no one really cared to tried. The mother-son duo spent their days talking about things like pretty colors and patterns on sarees and how they gleamed when the sun shone over them. The perfect talking point for the weaver and the "seer."

Months passed by and winter slowly rolled in. Summers were fierce in Olasigh and so were the winters. It would get dark earlier, so Sona and Ranju would try to wrap up all chores as quickly as they could and retire home for a hot meal. Ranju's blurry vision had become a constant by then and it had almost stopped bothering him. He soaked in the blurry versions of the roads, trees, faint outlines of people and was happy with his version of the world. It seemed warmer and more accommodating.

On one such winter morning, Ranju woke up or so he thought. He opened his eyes, but it seemed like he was still asleep but with no dream playing. There was complete darkness. Pitch black. It took his young, befuddled mind a couple of seconds to understand what might have happened. The moment the reality of blindness hit him; he was lost. He was lost in his own home, in his own bed. He was not ready for this. He had not expected this. It took him about two minutes to realise what to do next, which was, of course, screaming at the top of his lungs calling out for his mother.

Sona, who was outside washing utensils, came running inside. She saw Ranju with his eyes wide open, screaming and shouting, "*Maa, Maa*...I can't see a thing!" tears rolling down his cheek, thick and steady. Sona was shocked. She ran to her son and hugged him tightly, screaming the names of all the

Gods Whom she could remember at the unfortunate moment. Praying to them for mercy on her son, she ran helter-skelter stuffing in food, money, and clothes in a bag to rush Ranju to the eye doctor. Ever since Ranju stopped complaining about his blurry vision, Sona had heaved a sigh of relief, but little did she know that her little prince was trying to save her from trouble.

Sona and Ranju set off to see Dr. Mishra, a renowned eye specialist in the nearby town. Their five hours of bus journey, filled with anxiety and a glimmer of hope brought them to Mayapur, the town where Dr. Mishra resided and practised. They rushed to the small, unassuming clinic and upon describing the nature of emergency were soon whisked into the doctor's chamber. Upon examination, Dr. Mishra concluded that it was a case of congenital glaucoma, which meant that Ranju had this condition since birth but never truly realised its severity. Dr. Mishra said he could treat the condition, but it would require surgery and a good amount of pre and post treatment and preparation. Sona was aghast. Ranju had stopped listening. Mother and son left the doctor saying they will be back soon and boarded the next bus back to Olasingh.

It would take Sona at least five months to collect the money required for the surgery. While she started working double shifts to arrange the money as quickly as possible, Ranju started spending more time alone at home trying to figure out ways to go about household chores, using his other four senses. His daily tête-à-tête with the sun had, as expected, stopped. Not because he had lost hope but because he was now more focused on how to make life easier for his mother. He spent every waking moment trying to get work done at home. Going to school was not an option anymore. A stickman who couldn't see was an obvious bully magnet and since he couldn't see, he wouldn't be able to study at school either.

Ranju did what he could do staying at home. He started praying ardently. He closed his eyes shut and prayed to the Gods to help his mother and keep her happy. He did this regularly and sometimes for hours to end. Little did Ranju know that what he had actually started doing was meditating at the altar of the universal Almighty, prayers to Whom seldom go unanswered.

Many a time, while meditating Ranju would see a spark of light emanating and filling up the otherwise dark space he had learned to live in. This amazed him. Soon he started looking forward to the moments he spent in silent prayer and tried to get drenched in every bit of that light he could see with his closed eyes.

One morning, Ranju woke up with a searing headache. Just as he started wondering what could be worse than blindness that could be causing this, he realised that his vision had returned. He could see everything around him and this time his vision was not blurred. Instead, it seemed like he was looking at everything through a shiny, white, transparent veil. He rushed to his mother who upon listening to this news, felt life return to her otherwise dead self. Sona decided it would be better to take Ranju to Dr. Mishra for a checkup and ensure that the loss of eyesight did not relapse again.

Their journey uptown was uneventful but full of excitement. Ranju soaked in every bit of sight he could and, of course, greeted his old friend the Sun, with a warm smile after a long time. Once they were in town, they saw the doctor. Ranju walked into the chamber on his own, without any assistance.

"Are you sure you can see, Ranju? Tell me what's written in the fourth line of the board in front of you?" the doctor asked after conducting an initial examination.

"LPED" Ranju replied quickly, reading from the board placed afar.

The doctor seemed thoroughly confused. He carried out some more tests and examinations and seemed to be getting more addled, every time.

"His sight has still not returned, Sona." Dr. Mishra told the bewildered mother, "at least, not per my diagnosis. They still show the same damage that I had seen last time you were here. And to tell you the truth, I have never come across anything like this before."

The doctor then scribbled the name of Dr. Acharya, a famous eye surgeon who practised in Bhubaneshwar and asked Sona to take Ranju to him.

Neither Sona, nor Ranju could understand what had happened. While on their way back to Olasingh, they both decided to give this newfound vision a shot before consulting Dr. Acharya. After all, whether or not medical science approved of this, Ranju could now see and that is what mattered the most. It must have been God's grace that had returned his sight to him.

Mother and son chattered happily on their way back and Sona soon fell asleep. Relief had overcome her after a long time, and she snoozed away like a baby. Ranju sat there, enjoying the changing views and looking at his mother, adoring her every now and then.

The bus soon stopped, and a man of about 30 years of age boarded the bus with his old father. The son seemed terribly upset. Ranju kept looking at the two, trying to figure out what might have happened. The son soon broke down in tears and the father tried his best to console him. The son in a strange manner seemed oblivious to the presence of his father next to him. This seemed odd to Ranju. He knew that if he could ever have his father back, he would hug him so tight and would never let him leave, ever again. This man, however, did not share the same thought, Ranju felt.

This scene lasted for a good fifteen minutes, till the bus halted at the next stop, Rangpur, and another young man boarded the bus. He looked around for seats on the bus and realized there were none left except maybe one. The young man started walking up towards the man who was crying a river now and bent down to sit next to him. Before Ranju could even decipher what was happening, the father disappeared into thin air and the young man took the seat.

A wave of nausea hit Ranju and he started feeling dizzy. His hands turned cold. He closed his eyes and opened them again to the same silvery veil of vision he had been seeing. Little did the angelic boy know that he had indeed been given the gift of vision. The vision, unattainable for any eye on earth…the vision of the third eye.

*A sphere shaped, orange coloured sweet, made of flour, *ghee*, and sugar.

Those Rusted Lines

by Pratyay Ganguly

"If there is one thing that I want you to remember…

Remember my love…that I was right here, standing in front of you with my eyes drenched in the tears of a blissful love and you too… were right here, tightly clasped in my arms; our bodies shivering in the sudden winds of destiny as we both held each other close, for eternity. The stars smiled from above, the wind jeered in my ears as I could feel the slow silent ripples of your warm love over the cold black waters of my dark and desolate soul.

Remember my love…that no matter what happens, I will always be there to hold you in times of your trouble…and as the clock itself gets paused by one kind touch of the small petite intricately adorned fingers of life…I will always rest my head deep upon your breasts, smile and then heave large heavy breaths of a vindictive emancipation deep onto your blood and your bones.

And that's why, as I get the silent slow calls of the Satan himself onto his heavenly burrow, I hereby leave for you, the most cherished gifts of my life – the empire of my dreams. Take this empire my love, and promise me that no matter what happens, you'll always remember me.

Remember my eyes, remember my dark chiseled chins of time. And amongst all the ubiquitous demonic collisions of the egotist superpowers of the world, promise me, that you'll always remember to find my voice...my face...the sound of my laughter camouflaged deep beneath the shadows of the everlasting joys and sorrows of life, because, my love...you were my shackles of despondence and you yourself, my wings of an ecstatic redemption!

My love... I have loved you enough...enough...such that no mortal being can do ever do to anyone else in this world...so that no death... ever... can do us apart.

Remember me my love....remember...."

I closed the diary, kept it on the side table overshadowing under the maroon table lamp and took a deep sip on my fair share of the black liquid from the glass on my side. A pause came down inside the room, their silent lines of indignation cutting deep through the hearts of all the four of us, tearing apart all the blank desolate spaces inside our own blood and bones with an apprehensive bunch of solemn harsh truths. The cold rum made the way of its ravaging flames through my gut, connecting across all the thin dots inside my body, as I waited, patiently, for their slow elevated touches of a sweet pain of transcendental bureaucracy onto all of my senses. I waited patiently, for those rusted words to keep their eternal promise, made out of the silent conversations between my heart and the ever smiling hands of the clock. These were like the millionth time I read those lines from his diary, and yet the feelings always feels nascent each and every single time.

"Amazing man. This was written by your uncle na, Avinash?"

I looked straight at Ritu and nodded my head.

"Yes."

"When is it dated?", Anirban asked from my right.

"14th July, 1971."

I couldn't exactly remember how many times I have read those lines alone in public, so that now, every detail of it had been learnt by me by heart!

"Your uncle didn't marry, did he?" He asked again.

I took another sip on my drink.

"Nah. As far as I know, these writings have been found from his house just a day after the police hunted him down, first tortured him to his limits and then encountered him near the Ahiritola ghat. My mother found these out and she kept all of it to her. She didn't even utter a single thing when the police questioned about her only brother's left out documents and papers. It was only just a couple of years ago that I had found them inside mom's trunk."

"I …I am sorry…but why was your uncle encountered, Abhi?"

I looked straight at the person sitting at the rightmost corner of the black sofa inside my drawing hall. Wearing a pink kurti and a cream colored leggings, Sohini was looking straight at me, her eyes moist with the linings of a mystique mixture of an addictive kohl of restraint and composure. The next moment, out of nowhere a cold chill went down my spine and numbed all of my senses. She looked… beautiful!

"Abhi's uncle was a Naxal leader Soh, a prime name in Uttar Kolkata in the early 70's." Anirban whispered out the words from my right.

"Oh…ok."

I saw her face to droop down a little. Being in a relationship with Anirban for only a couple of months now, this was naturally new news to her. And from the look of her face I could properly guess that she didn't even like what she heard. After a moment, my instincts were corrected.

"I am sorry to hear that, Abhi. But," she paused to look at me, "Can I tell you something?"

At once I recognized those eyes as I looked straight at her. I knew them. They were etching across their limits.

"I don't think they did a very good deal, Abhi."

"I..I am sorry..what?"

She finished her whiskey and then kept her glass on the side table.

"I am not saying that their intention wasn't good, but the implementation – it was horrific! I mean, no revolution can be successful when it involves the mass murder of innocent peoples and strikes an intense fear of survival inside the hearts of the common."

"Are you saying that you don't support the ideology of Naxal Movement, Soh?" Anirban's eyes rung with disbelief.

"No." She paused to look at Ani. "I am saying I don't support its strategy and implementation. And that's it."

Another pause fell upon the room. I stood up from my ground and treaded my steps slowly towards my balcony. Being a cold December night, it was characteristically awfully quiet, and even from this far, I could hear the sirens of a ship far away into the abyss. Maybe, it was leaving the shore. Or was it just a warning sound?

"Abhi…you ok?" Ritu's voice came out like a whisper into my ears.

"Of course!", I smiled. "I mean I know what happened was very cruel indeed, but I have never even met that man! So, forget about it now. The past is past, there is no point brooding over it. Now tell me," I roamed around to face her.

"How's your relationship going with Imran?"

No sooner had I said those words, than a flash of color drained out from her face as her expressions changed. The next second, Ritu's head drooped down. From the corner of my eyes I looked at Ani. He was looking at Ritu. His eyes, inquisitively invigorating.

"Everything good, Ritu?"

Ritu looked up to face me.

"It's going good Abhi, but I am very scared for us!"

"Why?" This time it was Anirban.

Ritu looked first towards him and then at her glass.

"Imran's father have a very strong ideology about his religion. Many times in his life he has heard his father telling both him and his sister, Isha , that no matter what happens, he won't let them get married to any Hindu. Such is his anger towards Hindu that Imran is dead scared of even telling him about us!"

"Hmmm…."

I looked at the faces of both of my childhood friends. First at Anirban and then at Ritu.

"Ritu, don't you think it's time that he should tell his father about you guys? We are about 28years old now. I mean, let's admit the truth much too soon we all are going to get married." No matter I said those words than Sohini's eyes connected with me. But only for a split second. The next, I didn't dare anymore!

Ritu looked up towards me. And even in the thin faint yellowish lights of the vapor lamp, I could see her eyes. They were moist. And from her look, I could properly guess that she was indeed hiding something from us. But what?

"Well, Ritu, if you ask my opinion, I must say that I support your father's decision."

What? All the other three pairs of eyes roamed towards the person sitting on the bean bag at the rightmost corner of the room just beside Sohini, wearing a black shirt and light faded denims.

"Excuse me, what did you say just now?"

Sohini's disbelief rung in her voice as she looked at her boyfriend.

Anirban looked first at Sohini and then at Ritu. Then , when he spoke, his voice sounded much too embellished.

"Look Ritu, I know I may sound way too orthodox here, but look at this side, will ya? Imran has been raised entirely differently from us. His cultures, his views , his ideologies everything regarding his religion is way too different from the way we see it. And if someday or the other, you try to make him understand that all of the religion are equal in every way, will he be able to understand that? Even a tiny bit? I mean…come on Ritu! It's marriage we are talking about!"

A silent pause came down on the room yet again. This time, Sohini was the one who broke it.

"Of all the time that I have known you, I didn't know that you hated Muslims this much, Ani."

"Oh! Come on Soh…I don't hate them!" Ani's voice rose. "I never said I hate people just because of their religion. I hate people whom I don't like, not religions! I have many of my best friends who are Muslim! That's not even the question. I am just saying that being good friends is nice, but when it comes to marriage, I think we all should give it a second thought!"

Sohini continued to look at him, her eyes dripping with the invisible pearls of a deep indignation.

"So that means, if I would have been a Muslim, you wouldn't have been in a relationship with me?"

Ani looked at her face and then at mine. Then, very quietly, he relaxed back on his bag as he took another sip from his glass.

"This is not a situation for asking hypothetical questions about you Soh. It's about Ritu's life! I mean, her LIFE for God's sake!"

From far away, the siren of a ship came wailing onto my ears as I checked the clock. It was close to around 10'O clock in the night. Was it time yet? This early?

"I have thought about it all," Ritu took heavy breaths as she spurted out those words. "And if there comes any hindrance in my way, I am ready to adapt to the circumstances , however cruel they may be! But in no damn way am I going to lose Imran just over a petty thing as religion!"

"What? Ritu? What if…what if your in-laws tell you not to go outside the house without wearing a burkha? Or worse, what if, they…they want you to change your own religion?"

Ritu looked at Ani. And from this far, I could properly guess that her lips were shivering with the amplified clouds of desperation fuelled by the fire of a despotic arrogance.

"Then, I'll do it."

"WHAT?! What the…..Ani first looked at her and then at me. Abhi, tell her something Abhi. Make her understand that what she is thinking of doing is very wrong. It's wrong for her family for God's sake!"

I kept looking at Anirban from far, and then at Sohini. She was looking at me!

The next moment, suddenly, Ritu stood up.

"Ok, now it's time! I know I should have told you guys before, but I couldn't find a chance to do so until now. So, here it is! I am meeting Imran at Gariahat More tomorrow in front of the marriage registrar's office." She looked at me. "We are getting married tomorrow, Abhi. Everything is planned, and immediately after the marriage we are planning to go to Dalhousie and stay there for at least a month. Working at the same office, our leaves has already been sanctioned accordingly, and we have already saved some money beforehand for the plans. Now only one thing remains. I need two witnesses."

She walked towards me and slowly, kneeled down in front of me. "Will you guys help me, Abhi?"

"What? NOO!" This time, it was Ani who jumped up from his seat. "You can't do this Ritu. YOU JUST CAN'T! I have known your for fourteen years now, and not a single time have I seen you this impulsive. Ritu, think about your parents! What will happen to them? Ritu…think for one more time GODDAMN IT!"

Ritu kept looking at me with broken eyes, not even flinching once at the words of Ani.

"I have done enough thinking Abhi. I can't live without him, Abhi. I cant live without Imran. I just cant…"

Anirban came from behind, held Ritu by her hands and pulled her towards him.

"Ritu…come to senses, Ritu. COME TO SENSE YOU MAD WOMAN!"

And a couple of jerks were all that she could take. Because after the third, when both of me and Sohini went to her rescue, she was already deep into Ani's arms, breaking down to her every cell as she burst out in tears.

I CAN'T LIVE WITHOUT IMRAN. I just can't. Why don't you guys understand WHY?…why..why…

For a couple of moments the universe paused itself as we both stood still to see a pair of arms hugging an estranged soul very tightly deep into his arms. Maybe, my vision got blurred for a second too, I don't know. Only a couple of moments that's all they got. Maybe, we could have given them a little more. But then again, we didn't!

Because the next, all the three of us hugged her as she continued crying to the deepest of her soul inside Ani's chest. Ani made helpless bewildered expressions as his eyes contacted with mine, but not for a single time he let her loose. And then, when all the rains of her heart were flooded on all of the elements of our friendship, she came out from Ani's chest, and looked dead towards me.

"Avi…you'll help me, don't you? Ani..Abhi you guys are the only ones that I have. Please help me, please. I am begging you…please…."

For a moment, both of us looked deep into her moist crimson eyes. Then, as I hugged her, I kept my right hand over her small cute head and ruffled her hair all along the way.

"Ritu, no matter what happens, we'll be always be there for you!"

Ritu looked towards Ani.

"And you Ani? Wont you be there at my side on the most prized day of my life?"

Ani looked deep into her eyes. Then, towards me.

"Ani? Tell me.."

"Yes, he will be there for you, Ritu." I said . The next moment, Ani left Ritu and went back to his place, dead silent.

"I will be there too!"

Sohini smiled at Ritu. And for the first time in the night, Ritu smiled at all of us.

"Really? Thank you sooo much. Ok, then! Will be meeting you all at 12'o Clock near Gariahat more tomorrow. Ok?"

The ideation of being married with the love of her life changed her mood in just an instant. She chirped, smiled as she went back to her place and took up her bag. Then she glanced at her brown leather wrist watch.

"Thanks to uncle and aunty Avi, that they have gone to their relatives place tonight, otherwise I don't know when we would have met next! Now, it's already forty minutes past ten. I must be at home tonight. Because from tomorrow…." She paused in her sentence, thought about something, and then a deep shadow crossed her face as she smiled amongst all her clouds.

"Good night ,Abhi, Ani." She then turned towards her. "Sohini, you stay near Lake Gardens, right? Come I'll drop you".

"Ok."

Both of the girls got ready to leave, and just when Sohini was ready with her belongings and was just about to disappear behind the main door, she turned around.

"Abhi?"

I paused between the drags of my smoke.

"Yes?"

I loved your uncle's writing. Then, her voice changed.

"Will you please recite it to me the next time I come here, Abhi?"

This time, it was my turn to smile amongst the dense hazy clouds of my heart.

"Sure. Good night!"

"Good night."

She smiled and disappeared behind the door.

"Abhi, I am coming in a bit."

"I know." I looked at Ani. "Take your time. OK?"

"Ok."

All the three of them disappeared behind the door as I kept it open and again went towards my balcony. A minute later, all I could see was the brown striped hair of Sohini, flying in the wind way deep down into the abyss. The next, just before entering into the cab, I saw her to shift her gaze and look up towards my balcony. And exactly at that moment, it happened.

A clear sound of a siren came flying across the wind only to make its place deep inside my heart. Ani was still holding her hands, and from up it all looked like a mirage of a thousand splendid dreams, waiting to be brought to life by one cruel touch of a falsified truth.

A truth, that neither of us could even imagine, but now, we had no other choice but to accept it!

Finally, it was the time of my Armageddon to set in!

The ship picked up its anchor and got ready to sail towards its destination.

This time, it's voyage for the eternal was waiting for a promise made all across the dense dark waters of its destiny.

And as their cab started and made their way out of my vision, only one thing roamed inside my mind, making me smile on my own.

The ship forgot to mention her return date.

Or maybe, she didn't want to make any such promises!

It was a fact.

I mean, why would she?

After all, she was destined for another harbor, not mine!

The next moment, I felt a lump inside my throat as I looked deep down again at the streets.

Even in the dull hazy sodium vapour lights of the street, I could still see him.

His head was buried deep inside his chest as he stood still, like a painting made to come to life by one careless camaraderie of the rusted fingers of an artist; one who was drawn only, to stand alone, silhouetting the dark canvas of a desolate night for a millions of lifetime.

He was like me!

He was like a warrior who had been defeated by the cruel denigrating swords of time.

Like a friend, who had lost everything in his life.

Like a lover, who had lost the love of his entire life in just a night into the hands of a man who was not only a challenge but also one who questioned the very existence and the religion of her love.

Or maybe it was all my mistake!

No matter the events of the past few hours, I knew deep down that love is the only one thing in this mighty universe, which cares a damn about anything, let alone religion!

I silently traced my way back into my room as I knew the warrior standing all alone in the empty battlefield ten floors down from me needed some time now for himself.

After all, he had lost the battle without even a single fight.

I knew my friend from my heart.

I knew…that Ani was crying!

I have known Sohini for three years now. She works with me at my office but we bonded more because like me, she was also a passionate writer in her free times - poetry being her main genre. Ani had met her at one of my office parties and he liked her ever since. And the day I decided to tell her about my feelings, quite coincidentally, Ani had proposed her and she had accepted it in one go! Just like that!

Sometimes now, by the look on her eyes, I can feel that she loves Ani. Maybe, me..too? I don't know!

Suddenly I felt bad about her. She was such a nice woman. But did she know Ani to the fullest? Did she know the man and the one, whom he truly loved?

Indeed Ani liked Sohini. It was only three months that he had met her and things were really pacing fast and then, right when he was sure he was about to get over her, Ritu announced her marriage that night! And that too, a secret one. Ani was always envious of Imran, or what he liked to say, 'that pervert Muslim office boss of hers' for the last two years that they had been in a relationship. It was about much later when I understood that the actual reason for Ani's hatred towards such a pleasant and a talented guy like him was not because of his religion, but because of the priceless possession he had held very tightly in his fingers when we had met him for the only time in this last couple of years - Ritu's soft gentle hands.

Yes, Ani loved Ritu. Ani loved her way too much, right from our childhood days when we three used to study and play together but not even for a single time, could confess his feelings to Miss Rituparna Ganguly, aka our own Ritu. I don't know why, but when I think about it now, I can't blame him too much for that! After all, love is a feeling that is meant to be cherished deep inside the hearts that feels it, not to be used as a symbol of flamboyance or desperation, isn't it?

Though he didn't ever know of my feelings towards Sohini (and he won't, ever), I knew about his feelings for Ritu for the last five or six years, and also the fact that Ritu never considered him anything more than just a good friend! But, I never said anything. Deep inside, I knew one day or the other Ani will come out of the closet and open his heart to Ritu, but… There was a time when, in my solitary nights, I used to ask myself the question, that would there have been any change of circumstances even if Ani did express his love to her? Even if Ani told Ritu that he has been in love with her since…ever?

Nowadays I have stopped asking that question! Not because it doesn't come in my mind anymore, but because I know the answer and truly speaking, I am too scared to accept it!

Everything went into that night. That night, when, after returning nearly about an hour later after Ritu and Sohini had departed. Ani broke down on my sofa; and amongst all his silent screams and despaired attempts to fulfill his despotic love for Ritu, I held him tight as he plunged his head deep into my chest, shivered intermittently and wanted to hear only those lines, again and again, until his tears got soaked up all dry on time and his mind, slowly, got cleared of the obnoxious cloud of a mortified unimagined redemption; a redemption that he had to be the witness of the marriage of the girl, that he had loved, ruthlessly, for the last fifteen years of his life!

And as his inebriated mind and lips twitched and turned in agony of losing the love of their lives to someone else, I stayed calm and still, with my vision blurring the world outside my senses more and more as I read those rusted lines again and again, that my uncle had jotted down in his brown diary of imagination.

The lines, that he had written for his country.

Yes, I have never met my uncle. I don't know whether he would have liked to see me, his only nephew accepting life as it comes to him. He himself didn't, and that's why he turned into a revolutionary to change the country to one that he had dreamt of, isn't it?

A country for which he was so romantic, that it got his name engraved into the invisible dusts of time inside the list of millions of martyrs who had thrown themselves into the fire just because they couldn't accept the way life was back then!

The country to which he gave away his everything.

The country, that gave him a worthy return gift for his love.

She took his life like a rodent and dumped his body into the filth of a mental abyss! Ha!

His only fault?

He , like a million others , dreamt of a country where all people should be treated equally, in every way!

Communist they say! Ha! I smiled as I said those words again, in my mind.

Communism is a myth! There won't ever be any equality in this world. Not until love is alive in this planet. And that means, not for eternity!

Sometimes now, I feel it was for the best of my stars that I wasn't born at your times, uncle. You know why? Because neither do I have the courage to throw myself into the fires of such a romantic imagination like you did, nor do I have the guts to betray you guys and tell all your whereabouts to the authority! I loved your romanticism uncle, but I am sorry to say, I couldn't even dream to be a part of it!

You can call me a coward for that, I don't mind. After all, I accept life as it comes to me, and to you revolutionaries, that's the most simplified definition of a 'coward', isn't it, uncle?

But what can I say? Contentment and injustice doesn't go hand in hand, but life…does!

Long live your revolution uncle!

Long live your vengeance!

We are all waiting for you to rise up once again from your ashes!

And maybe you don't know this, but we have also started a revolution within our own selves, uncle.

Our revolution is one of Silence!

Our arms are made of maimed hearts and moist tears!

Our dream of a country? One where we always get to respect light and time, the two inseparable elements of life and destiny!

What did you say? A revolution can't take place without fires and gunshots?

Ha! Uncle! I don't know where you are, but I wish you could have seen me right now. I wish you could come and have a look at the twenty-eight year old guy clenching my shirt right now as he is crying his hearts out inside of me. He is crying uncle, for his loss! And here I am, silently soaking all his tears, not even flinching for a single moment, in the dream of a benevolent future; a future that can be brought to us by saying those words inside my head again and again like a hymn to a deity –"What happens, happens only for the good! Whatever has happened, happened only for the good! Whatever will happen, will also happen for ...."

I wish you could understand our language of revolution uncle!

I wish, I could have showed you my own language of tears inside your chest, wither in pain and tear your heart in pieces like Ani is doing, right now, to me!

But alas…it's all a myth now!

Because you have given up your life for this country!

Sometimes, come visit us when you can, will you?

This country needs you now more than ever.

This frenzied society is in dire need of the blazing warmth of all of your imaginative romanticism more than ever!

Peoples like Ritu and Imran needs you.

Ani needs you!

I….need you…uncle.

I…need….

Finally, when I went to bed that night, just before dozing off to sleep beside my maimed asleep friend, I said those exact same words in my mind, that Ani made me recite again and again as his agony shed tears of despondence deep inside my chest. And that's exactly when, a pair of bright eyes flashed in front of me like a mirror of all of the truths of my life.

Suddenly I could see it!

There it is. A white cruise ship, floating across the shore over the small dark blue benevolent tides of time, intermittently blowing the sirens of a mutilated life deep into the heart of a loner called the city of Kolkata on a dark cold December night as it waited to start its voyage towards the unknown.

And then, she slowly picks up its rusted anchor and starts to sail on her way as I stand there, all alone, smiling, waving my handkerchief high up in the air in a silent valediction as it dripped wet with the blood of all my prerogatives lashed onto a cruel death by the immoral hands of an integral antagonist of life destiny!

A deep smile sketches across my heart as I see the name of the ship.

There she is. A pair of eyes , smiling at me from its top deck.

The eyes, that I had even caught a few hours ago, stealing glances of me.

Those eyes, that meant everything for me.

Slowly and slowly she fades into the darkness of the sea on to the point where the color of her ruffling red sari gets matched up with that of the darkness of the surroundings…and…and the last time I saw her, she smiled and waved her fingers at me in a blatant goodbye. And then, she was gone!

"…you were my shackles of despondence and you yourself, my wings of an ecstatic redemption .

My love… I have loved you enough…enough…such that no mortal being can ever do in this world…so much so that no death… ever… can do us apart…

Remember me my love…."

Remember me….communism…

Remember me….revolution…

Remember this coward…Sohini…

Remember…me …will you?!

…Please?!

The Walls Have Ears

by Manali Desai

The lights blinked blood red across the entire street. So much so that even the walls of the crammed up houses appeared red, even though the lighting inside the house was not so.

As I walked deeper into the infamous Kamathipura district of Mumbai I could slowly grasp why it was called the 'Red Light' district of the 'City of Dreams'. In a city that claimed to never sleep, this street and its notorious activities were surely one of the reasons Mumbai had been so named.

From the fullfigured to the scrawny, I could see women of all shapes, trying to lure men and women alike into their abodes with promises of a night to be remembered. "What am I doing here?", I asked myself for the umpteenth time as I realized how unwelcome and unbelonging I felt at this place.

The stories around Kamathipura had intrigued me right from the time I had read my first book chronicling the city and its tales of crime, darkness, poverty, corruption and prostitution. As a teenage reader, the roles played by these ***fallen*** women in capturing and bringing down some of the most wanted and dangerous criminals, had actually made me look upon them as heroes rather than whores.

I had been mustering up the courage to walk down this street ever since my first encounter of such a reading. "What kind of lives must these women lead?" "Why do they do what they do?", and "What must their families be like?", these kinds of questions took seed in my ever curious mind which only grew curiouser with age.

As a teenager, I was pretty sure I would never be allowed entry here; even mentioning the name of this place in front of my parents would have led to uncomfortable questions and ugly confrontations. Not to mention, I myself was meek and shy to have taken up the courage to enter it at that point of time in my life.

But, having been through quite a few ups and downs in my own life and still trying to get the whole adulting process right, I was sure this was something I just had to do! As to the 'why I wanted to do it' and 'what was I doing here', I was still not sure.

After months of justifying and gruelling with my own thoughts, I had taken the leap today and was here. But now that I literally stood at the crossroads, I didn't know what to do. As I observed the women, either standing outside their homes, or strolling on the streets or casually chatting among themselves, I again battled with my courage on walking up to them and having a chat. I took up the street view up and down once more, observing the cheap makeup and clothes the women had put on, took a deep breath and walked closer to one of the women who had been eyeing me curiously from quite some time.

This woman (or girl, as I wasn't sure of her age thanks to the thick makeup and her ample bosom which I could only dream of having) had a long sharp nose, luscious lips and an hourglass body. Just two steps away from her now, I conjured up a greeting I thought would be appropriate, but once I reached there and extended my hand to her, the words that blurted out of my mouth were, "**I want to be like you**".

Mentally kicking myself on such an inappropriate statement and introduction, I did some damage control by saying, "I am so sorry. Hi, my name is Damini."

Eyebrows arched and mocking, the woman in front of me said in a tone which immediately implied a come hither invitation, "Damini? Like that Bollywood movie? And I thought we're the filmi ones!" I simply smiled on that comment and asked, "What is your name? I would like to know more about you".

She laughed derisively and replied, "My name is Simran. *Naam toh suna hoga?* She chuckled at her own joke and continued, "What do you want to know? Why do I do this? Have you come to rescue me from this gutter as so many of you high class people seem to think and promise?"

I was shocked at her bluntness but soon recovered and said as politely as I could, "No ma'am (anything to make her less intimidating). I am only here to get to know about you and your life." She looked me up and down and seemed to assess whether I was pulling off some sort of a joke. When I refused to budge from my place and kept my face as nonchalant as possible, she sighed, turned around and called out, "Bindu, Anjali, Laila, Pooja, Nisha, Paro, Chandramukhi, Sridevi, Madhuri....Come here all of you"

Before I could ponder about the Bollywoodishness of all the names she had just called out, Simran gauged my expression and clarified, "No, these aren't our real names. Most of our clients fantasize about sleeping with Bollywood actresses so we cleverly pick a pseudo name around popular heroines and their most sensational movie characters. This way they're already half convinced to sleep with us once we've told them our name and before we go on to discuss our hourly or nightly charges."

I nodded over the ingeniousness of this, as about 8 to 10 women gathered around me and Simran in the next minute or so. All of them had the same mocking or curious expression as their eyes first scanned me and then turned questioningly to Simran. As if she was giving them time to assess the situation on their own, Simran waited before she addressed them and said, "This is Damini. Much like the movie she seems to be named after, she's interested in getting to know about us and our lives." She made air quotes when she said, *"getting to know"*, which made the women around us smirk and some even laughed out loud.

A voluptuous, short woman, with dusky skin and whose eyes somehow made me think of a vulture, who was standing next to Simran, whispered something in her ear. They both turned gravely towards me as Simran asked, "How can we trust you? What if you turn out to be a spy or someone working with the police?"

Now it was my turn to laugh and after I was done cackling over someone thinking about me as a policewoman, I answered, "Really? Well, I am flattered. But here's my phone. You can keep it, and this is my college ID. You can check my age. Not only am I much too young to be associated with any kind of police work but I'm also too naïve for any investigative work, which obviously you can guess from my venturing out here all alone."

Some women chuckled at this, and few still seemed sceptical, but most of them nodded their agreement on my response. Simran seemed convinced too, so taking the initiative, began her story as she said, "Well, mine would be the most cliched story. I got lost as a child. I had been visiting Bombay for the first time with my parents and brother. I was only 8 years old at that time. When we reached Victoria Terminus, while alighting the train from the unreserved class, in the ensuing crowd I lost grip of my mother's clutched hand. I shouted and cried for my mother, but there was no way for me to either get out of that crowd or to locate her in the mass of various body parts; all of which began to suffocate me. I was starting to feel faint, when I remember someone grabbing me and pulling me out of the carriage with their hands around me. A handkerchief'ed hand was hastily stuffed over my nose and the next thing I remember is waking up in Asha Tai's whorehouse which is where most young girls (she stopped here to clarify that by 'young' she meant 'virgin') are taken to, for selling off to the highest bidder. I was taken that night itself. I begged and begged for Asha Tai to let me stay but she just watched as he dragged me to a dirty, dimly lit room. All I remember after that, is crying out, sometimes in pain and mostly out of the unfairness of it all." She stopped and smiled, as if the recollection was nostalgic rather painful, and continued again, "Over the years, I tried many times to escape, sometimes in the middle of the night and sometimes by vainly trying to track down my lost family, but soon realized that there was no way out of this hellhole, which funnily enough, I have now come to accept as home."

I don't know what surprised me more in Simran's story; whether the sheer physical and emotional pain she had to go through or just the matter of fact tone in which she narrated her story. The women around me seemed unmoved and as if on cue, the short, dusky woman next to Simran chimed in next, "My name is Madhuri. My parents dumped me as an infant in a dustbin. I'm guessing it was because they wanted a son and would rather have me dead than raise a daughter they didn't want in the first place. Unlike Simran, I didn't have a family, but Asha Tai raised me lovingly and I even began to consider her as my mother and my only family. That dream was soon shattered as I realized her true intentions of raising me well. I too was sold off, but at the age of 7. My virginity got the bitch a fat load of money too! I don't hold it against her anymore though because at least she didn't want me dead and she did what she had to. May her soul Rest in Peace."

A lot of the girls nodded at this and crossed their hearts, including Simran and Madhuri. I was intrigued as to how they could wish well on a dead soul who had ruined their lives. I was about to ask them this, when a fair complexioned, slim and tall girl, chirped, "To you all this may seem like a novelty. But for us, its routine life. All of us have similar stories including even Asha Tai. She may look villainous to you, but she did provide us a roof, shelter and in her own twisted way, a livelihood too."

As I looked around the walls of the house in whose veranda we were standing, I noticed a garlanded photo frame of a woman who could easily have been mistaken for Madhubala. Unbidding, a Hindi phrase came to my mind and I mumbled, *"Deewaro ke bhi kaan hote hai"* which probably explained why these women spoke reverentially of a woman who I could only think of as tagging 'Cruella de Vil' from 101 Dalmatians. I had another lingering thought as I listened to more of their tales, "These walls would have more stories to tell than any woman here can ever narrate!" and suddenly I wished the walls really did have ears so I could absorb everything they had ever witnessed!

Whatever the case, I was no one to judge these women's lives and their choices or even their way of thinking, because it was impossible to do so in just a few hours, whereas they had lived in these conditions all their adult life (I, on the other was still grasping at straws in the adulthood section anyway)

I walked out of that place, having my thirst for knowledge satiated but my curiosity on life, people and the unpredictability of it all, still unanswered at large. Undoubtedly, the women had left an unforgettable impact on my mind and my heart, but I was pretty sure they'd forget me before yet another 'red day' ended for them.

About the Authors
Proma Nautiyal

Entrepreneur and writer, Proma Nautiyal speaks four languages, fluently, and is a rare mix of logic and fantasy. She feels the phrase 'paradox personified' describes her the best. She embarked on a soul quest at a young age and her literary works often show expression of the same. Proma juggles marketing plans and business negotiations during the day, leaves on soul searching expeditions at night, and writes during the time between. Her keen observation helps weave life into the stories she authors, while her unique perspective gives the readers something most hope for in a story; hope, and intrigue.

Pratyay Ganguly

Words have always been the best of his friends right from his childhood days as Pratyay was raised in the addictive city of Kolkata. An engineer-turned author, Pratyay has been following his passion for writing along with pursuing a government job for long and around October this year, his story, 'Metamorphosis' got selected for the first time among others from authors all across the world, published by the prestigious publishing house 'Ukiyoto Publishing' in the book 'Ten Tales'.

Apart from writing, Pratyay is a singer, songwriter a composer as well as a lyricist having a Youtube channel of his own.

Manali Desai

After completing her MBA (as any good child should) and working in Marketing, Manali would jot down her thoughts (the ones about her boss, the traffic, or the solace she found in a piece of Kit-Kat after a long day) Soon, bored by her job, she decided to study the written and spoken word as it gave her the most pleasure! So, she did her MA in English Literature and taught English for a while, sharing her love for language with eager recipients. Still, something tugged at her heart strings. That's when she took the plunge and decided to go into fulltime writing. Currently a freelance writer and a blogger, she is a regular contributor to various national as well as international blogs and webzines and alongside these, even runs her own blog. A published poet with her poetry collection titled A Rustic Mind (available on Amazon Kindle), Manali enjoys spending her free time poring over books and pondering about life, alongside some good music and a cup of hot chocolate. Manali is a wanderlust by heart and travelling is her biggest muse which inspires her to write travel stories. A flamboyant wordsmith who passionately captures candid moments, Manali, on the path to follow her passion, has whipped up colors that have painted the town colourful.

You can connect with Manali or follow her works on social media platforms through the links below:

arusticmind.com *arusticmind*
a_rustic_mind

Write to her at manali1988@gmail.com *or* arusticmind@gmail.com

www.ingramcontent.com/pod-product-compliance
Lightning Source LLC
LaVergne TN
LVHW041554070526
838199LV00046B/1967